D0626940

Mia Can See Patterns

Written by Margo Gates

Illustrated by Carol Herring

GRL Consultants, Diane Craig and Monica Marx, Certified Literacy Specialists

Lerner Publications ◆ Minneapolis

Note from a GRL Consultant
This Pull Ahead leveled book has been carefully designed for beginning readers. A team of guided reading literacy experts has reviewed and leveled the book to ensure readers pull ahead and experience success.

Lerner Publications Company
A division of Lerner Publishing Group, Inc.
241 First Avenue North
Minneapolis, MN 55401 USA

For reading levels and more information, look up this title at www.lernerbooks.com.

Main body text set in Mikado 24/41
Typeface provided by Hannes von Doehren.

Photo Acknowledgments **DEC 1 2 2019**
The images in this book are used with the permission of: Carol Herring

Library of Congress Cataloging-in-Publication Data

Names: Gates, Margo, author. | Herring, Carol, illustrator.
Title: Mia can see patterns / by Margo Gates ; illustrated by Carol Herring.
Description: Minneapolis : Lerner Publications, [2020] | Series: Science all around me (Pull ahead readers-Fiction) | Includes index.
Identifiers: LCCN 2018056977| ISBN 9781541558519 (lb : alk. paper) | ISBN 9781541573345 (pb : alk. paper)
Subjects: LCSH: Readers (Primary) | Pattern perception—Juvenile fiction.
Classification: LCC PE1119 .G3846 2020 | DDC 428.6/2—dc23

LC record available at https://lccn.loc.gov/2018056977

Manufactured in the United States of America
1 – CG – 7/15/19

Contents

Mia Can See Patterns

Mia can see dots.

Mia can see stripes.

Mia can see ovals.

Mia can see lines.

Mia can see webs.

Mia can see patterns.

Did You See It?

dots

lines

ovals

stripes

webs

Index

16